CARNACKI

The Larkhill Barrow

Three Carnacki: Ghostfinder Stories

William Meikle

CONTENTS

THE BLOODED IKLWA 7

THE LARKHILL BARROW 29

THE SISTERS OF MERCY 53

FURTHER READING 77

The Blooded Iklwa

Carnacki's card of invitation arrived just as I was leaving for work on Friday and I had the whole weekend to wonder what tale he would have to relate this time. On Monday evening I arrived at seven o'clock prompt at his lodgings in Chelsea at 427, Cheyne Walk.

"How was Scotland?" I asked as I entered, but Carnacki merely gave me one of his trademark arch smiles and motioned me through to the parlour where I found the three others already there awaiting me.

It was not long before Carnacki, Arkwright, Jessop, Taylor and I were all seated at Carnacki's ample dining table.

As usual Carnacki would not discuss his latest adventure whilst dining, preferring to keep us waiting until we were ensconced in the parlour with some of his fine whisky and cigars. It was only once he was sure we were all settled that Carnacki lowered himself into his favourite chair, fired up his pipe, and began relating his latest adventure.

"As you may have heard from Dodgson, I have been in Scotland these past ten days," he began. "But the tale of how I came to be there is almost as interesting in itself.

"My story starts with a knock on the door of this very house eleven days ago.

"The man who stood on the doorstep was military through and through. His suit was thick worsted tweed, his regimental tie was knotted just right, and his brogues squeaked as he walked across the threshold. He was in his sixties, but held his back ramrod straight. He dyed his hair, but did a dashed good job of it, with just the right amount of grey showing at the temples and in his carefully-trimmed moustache.

"'My name is Captain James McLeod. I hear you deal in *mumbo-jumbo'*, he said as I closed the door behind him. 'I have a commission I would very much like you to undertake.'

"He had a slight Scottish brogue, but it was well disguised and I guessed he had spent years away from his homeland.

"Immediately after speaking he winced. I knew that expression -- this was a man in some degree of pain. I led him into this very parlour and poured him a large stiffener. He took to it like a man well used to the task. He sank a full two-thirds of the liquor before speaking.

"'Tell me Mr. Carnacki, do you know what an Ikwla is?'

"I did indeed.

"'It is a Zulu spear of some kind is it not?'

"He finished off the whisky in double quick time and I poured him another.

"He nodded his thanks, and I was pleased to note that he had the strength and fortitude to put his glass aside for a moment.

"'It is a thrusting weapon, a shorter version of the assagai. It gets its name from the sound a thrust makes, first as it enters a body and the moist sucking sound as it is withdrawn.'

"He punctuated his explanation with a thrusting motion of his own with his right hand, but had to curtail it when it brought with it another grimace of pain. He took to the whisky again before continuing.

"'I have some experience with such weapons,' he said

8

with a grim smile. 'I was at Uluni in seventy-nine, fighting under Chelmsford as an officer in the First King's Dragoon Guards.'

"The man's eyes took on a faraway stare, an old soldier remembering days of glory.

"'That was the day we broke the Zulu forever. I will not bore you with thirty-year old battles, but I rode off that field with a souvenir, an Iklwa that had pierced my thigh before I could cut down the wielder. Since my return to Scotland in eighty-seven it has been above the fireplace in my home. And there it stays. But I fear it has been travelling when no one is there to see.'

"My curiosity was piqued.

"'And why do you say that?'

"He lifted his waistcoat, and the shirt beneath. Below that was a bandage wrapped all around his body. A recent dark stain showed where he had exerted himself earlier and opened the wound below.

"'Three times now it has stabbed me while I lie abed," he said. "I have never seen the attack coming, nor been able to avoid it, even in a locked room. The iklwa is always above the fireplace in the morning. And blood adorns the blade.'

"He tucked his shirt back in place and straightened his tie.

"'What do you say Mr. Carnacki? Will you help me?'

"The next morning we took the *Flying Scotsman* to Edinburgh."

Carnacki stopped his tale to allow us time to refill our glasses and light another cigar or pipe as was our pleasure. We all knew better than to ask any questions at this stage of a story, and it was only a matter of a minute before we were once again settled and Carnacki took up from where he had left off.

"The Captain was a pleasant companion to have on the train. He regaled me with tales of his exploits in the Guards and proved most adept at bringing the sights and sounds of old battles to life.

"We reached Waverley Station at six-thirty in the evening, but our journey was not finished there, for the Captain's residence was outside the city. A carriage took us the rest of the way, a trip of nearly an hour, and it was full dark by the time we arrived at his handsome sandstone cottage.

"The Captain proved to be a gracious host. He had sent a telegram ahead, and his housekeeper had prepared a magnificent meal of salmon and pheasant, washed down with some strong Scotch ale. I was feeling pleasantly tired by the time the talk turned back to the Captain's predicament.

"He led me through to the parlour after dinner, and poured a large glass of whisky for each of us before pointing out the spear above the fireplace.

"'I can scarcely even look at the dashed thing,' the Captain said. 'Maybe I should just throw it in the river and be done with it.'

"At that I shook my head.

"'There is a puzzle here to be solved,' I replied. 'And I would be remiss in my duties if I did not attempt the resolution.'

"I walked over to the fireplace and made a closer study of the weapon. It was a short-shafted, large-bladed spear. Brass wire reinforced the socket, and it had a wood shaft below a foot-long steel blade. Its total length was some fifty inches overall. The blade itself showed no sign of rust, but there was a thin veneer of dried blood on the lower edge.

"I searched the fireplace and surrounding area thoroughly for any signs of trickery, but found none. That did not, of course, mean that no trickery existed. The Captain himself seemed rather fond of *a wee dram* and it is my experience that drink can do strange things to even the strongest of men.

"I also had the Captain show me his bedchamber. I could find nothing to suggest that the assaults on his person were staged by a human agent. A perusal of the door locks showed them to be sturdy and of high quality and the windows seemed to be of similarly sound construction. I was forced to agree with the man that we did indeed have a mystery on our hands.

"We repaired to the parlour for a final snifter. The Captain was destined for his bed, but I had another task in mind for myself. I waited until he had settled down for the night then placed an armchair outside his bedroom door, ensuring I had a view clear through to the parlour and the fireplace. I put out the lights and sat in the darkness smoking my pipe as silence fell all around me.

"There was just enough light for me to see the dying embers of the fire and make out the darker shadow above the mantle where the spear had been mounted. I knew that I would be unable to watch that shadow for every second, for the strain on my eyes would prove too much to bear. Nevertheless I was able to keep most of my concentration on the parlour itself, confident that if anything did indeed move that I would know of it in enough time to take action.

"The night passed slowly. I contented myself with running complex arithmetical problems in my mind, a soothing array of cube roots and prime numbers. I was almost lost in reverie when I noticed a drop in the temperature. Despite the fact that my pipe had long since gone out and grown cold, my breath smoked in front of my nose.

"The air grew thin, as if I had suddenly been transported to a high altitude, and a soft wind whistled at my ears.

"I peered into the darkness over the fireplace. The iklwa was still in its position, but the shadows seemed to have deepened around the fireplace, a blacker form above the mantle writhing like a nest of snakes. By Jove! You can imagine how queer I felt about *that*.

"I was just about to stand when a scream came from the Captain's room. By the time I threw the door open he was already sitting up in bed, bleeding profusely from a deep stab wound in his shoulder. Before I went to his aid I had a look back at the fireplace. The spear was still in position above the mantle.

"To his credit the old soldier did not make a fuss as I roused his housekeeper and between us we dressed the wound as well as we were able. The housekeeper, being one of that stoic breed of Scots women who treats everything with equal scorn, took over from my misplaced fumbling and banished me from *the maister's* room.

"I took the opportunity to have a closer look at the spear.

"It was right where it ought to be, still firmly secured above the mantle.

"Fresh blood dripped from the blade to the hearth below."

Carnacki stopped once more in his telling.

"Dodgson, can I bother you to fetch me a refill? I am finding this thirsty work."

I did as he requested. I poured him a large measure of his favourite single malt and set it on the small table by his side.

"I see your sojourn among the heathens to the north has

left its mark on you," I said jokingly.

The look he gave me showed how little he was amused by my remark.

"You are closer to the truth than you know," he said softly.

The others had taken advantage of the lull in proceedings to recharge their own glasses and to get fresh smokes lit. We sat contentedly in the growing fug waiting for the next revelation in Carnacki's story.

Carnacki got his own pipe lit before starting again. He showed us the long stemmed briar.

"I got a smoke lit and stood in that parlour for many minutes," he continued. "But no matter how I looked at it, I could come to only one conclusion. A revenant spirit was at work in this house, and it seemed intent on bringing harm, and maybe even death, to the old officer.

"I was about to check on his health when he arrived in the doorway. Apart from seeming slightly grey about the face he looked none the worse for wear, but there was a noticeable tremor in his hands as he poured us both a Scotch. If his own glass was more full than the one he passed to me, I chose not to mention it.

"It did not stay full for very long as he took a gulp that would have had me gasping on the floor. It did however succeed in bringing some colour back to his cheeks. He motioned towards the spear, not seeming to notice, or care, that some of the whisky slopped and spilled from his glass.

"'It seems I am to suffer the death of a thousand cuts. It was yon spear again,' he said, his accent stronger now than before. 'How in the duece is such a thing possible?'

"I took my time in replying, for in truth, I did not yet have any answers of my own to give. But I did know one thing.

"'The *how* of it is indeed puzzling,' I replied. "And that is something we need to settle very soon. But I believe there is an even more important question to be asked. *Why* are these attacks targeting only you? And why now, at such a distance from the battle in which you procured the spear?'

"Neither of us had an answer. The night was too far-gone, and we had too much liquor in our bellies. The Captain took to his bed once more, and I sat back in the armchair.

"And some point I slept, but my inexcusable laxity did not, fortunately, prove to be calamitous. The remainder of the night passed uneventfully, and I was woken to sunlight lancing across the parlour floor and the sound of the housekeeper ringing the breakfast bell.

"If the Captain was feeling any stiffness or pain from his new wound he did not show it at the table. He was a real *brick* about the whole thing. While the housekeeper fed us porridge, kippers and a mountain of toast he kept up a series of anecdotes about the social scene in Edinburgh that would have had the ears of the gentry in Morningside burning as they drank their morning tea.

"It was only after he was sure that his housekeeper was safely back in the kitchen washing the dishes that he turned to serious matters.

"He was looking for answers, but I did not yet have any to give. I did however have certain tricks up my sleeve. I banished the Captain to his club in the Castlegate and set to unravelling the mystery.

"First of all, in the clear light of day, I wanted to make sure, once and for all, that no human trickery was involved. I examined the parlour -- walls, floor and ceiling. I probed and hammered each and every piece of panelling and examined everything thoroughly through my magnifying glass. I found nothing suspicious. It was only after I was completely satisfied that I set to making preparations for the next night.

"I took my valise into the Captain's bedchamber. I had been sure to tell him of my plans that morning, for I was about to perform some acts that he would surely dismiss as *mumbo-jumbo*, and I needed his cooperation if we were to succeed.

"The Captain had retained his military regime and his bedchamber was little more than a bed and a dresser. I had little trouble in moving the bed into the centre of the room. Manhandling the dresser out into the hall was a different matter altogether. By Jove that thing was heavy. I worked up a sweat in no time, and needed a calming pipe of tobacco once the deed was done. Then it was swiftly back to work and to the *mumbo-jumbo* I have already mentioned.

"I started by drawing a circle of chalk, taking care never to smudge the line as I navigated my way around the bed. Beyond this I rubbed a broken garlic clove in a second circle around the first.

"When this was done, I took a small jar of water that had been blessed by a priest and went round the circle again just inside the line of chalk, leaving a wet trail that dried quickly behind me. Within this inner circle I made my pentacle using the signs of the Saaamaaa Ritual, and joined each Sign most carefully to the edges of the lines I had already made.

"In the points of the pentacle I placed five portions of bread wrapped in linen, and in the valleys five vials of the holy water. Now I had my first protective barrier and with this first stage complete the bed, now protected as it was by the most basic of spells, already felt more secure.

"I have told you enough tales by now for you to know

what I did next. I will not bore you with my reasons for utilizing the increased protection provided by my electric pentacle, for you know that it has saved me many times already, and proves most efficacious against even the most cunning apparitions. I set the mechanism to overlay the drawn pentagram upon the floor. When I connected up the battery, an azure glare shone from the intertwining vacuum tubes.

"By this time the stench of crushed garlic had assailed me enough. I made one final check that the protections were all in place then retired to the kitchen where the housekeeper provided me with coffee and gossip until the *maister* came home.

"That evening's meal proved every bit as welcome as the night before, but the Captain was more subdued, and loath to take to bed. I do believe he might have taken solace in the bottle had I not been present, and even then he took some convincing before finally retiring, muttering about *bloody heathen nonsense* as he stepped into the pentagram. I noticed however that he took pains not to stand on or smudge any of the lines.

"Once more I took to my watch in the armchair and the house went quiet around me as I puffed on a fresh pipe. Now that I had the protections set I felt more confident that I was ready for whatever the night might throw at me. I thought I knew what to expect.

"Indeed it began in much the same fashion as before. I can tell you that sheer funk almost took complete hold of me, sitting there in the dark. And when the air went cold I dashed near threw it all in there and then. But the thought of the old soldier lying abed just through the wall stiffened my resolve.

When the shadows grew above the fireplace and the wind whistled in my ears I knew that the time had come. I quietly opened the Captain's door and slid into the room.

"I was just in time to see a web of frost crawl across the window. The Captain himself was asleep and his breath was clearly visible in the sudden cold.

"A dark shadow ran around the walls, although there was no light from which it might have been cast. The wind in my ears grew stronger and the shadow *lunged* forward. It smashed against the protection in a shower of sparks. The pentacle held.

"Again and again the shadow forced an attack. Again and again it was repulsed by the pentacle until the attacks became an almost constant frenzy. It was quite a light show, I will say that much, although it was a tad cold for my tastes. I was just beginning to feel smug that my technology was proving a match for the *haunt* when the Captain woke with a start. He immediately made to climb out of bed and I could see that his foot would land square on one of the inner lines of the pentacle.

"I had no choice. I stepped forward, standing between him and the lowering shadow.

"The blackness came straight at me and a cold sharper than any I have ever felt gripped me down to my bones. Somewhere the Captain shouted but I was caught immobile in a cold dark place. The only heat came as a blade slid between my ribs and blood flowed freely.

"I fell to the ground, insensate."

Carnacki stopped in his telling and looked around at us. I followed his gaze and saw that the others were struck with the same dumb horror as I.

He laughed aloud.

"Do not worry yourselves unduly my friends," he said. "I am still alive."

He pulled up his shirt and showed us a white bandage that was wrapped around his body.

"But I am not yet fully well. I'm afraid I am too tired to finish the story tonight. But if we can meet again tomorrow evening, I can promise a conclusion to the tale."

We went out into the night with many unanswered questions, and only the hope that they would be answered on our return.

The next night began with an excellent meal of salmon that had been brought down on the *Scotsman* with Carnacki on his return. Once more he made us wait until the after dinner drinks before getting back to his tale, but he paid us the compliment of starting up immediately where he had left off.

"I woke just as the sun showed enough strength to melt the frost that was settled on the windows.

"I was lying on the Captain's bed. The old soldier and his housekeeper were both bent over me. The worried looks on their faces might almost have been comical in other circumstances. I tried to sit up, only to be rewarded with a hot pain in the ribs. The Captain gently pushed me back on the bed.

"'Rest man,' he said. 'You took a wound meant for me. The least I can do is lend you my bed for a while.'

"I leaned over enough to check the protections. All were still in place.

"They left me alone there in the room, and I slept the morning away. By the time the afternoon came around I was starting to feel like my old self and was able to rise and shuffle to the kitchen, only to be scolded like a miscreant child by the housekeeper. I talked her into providing coffee, and after I had a pipe-full of tobacco I felt greatly improved.

"The Captain had once more taken himself off to his club, so I used the afternoon in preparing for the night to come. Firstly I remade the pentacle. It took longer this time, for I was slowed by my injury, but eventually the job was done to my satisfaction once more. I knew that the protections worked against the *haunt*. Now it was time to answer some of our questions.

"I consulted the Sigsand MS on the matter of spells of revelation and was happy to find that I had all the necessary supplies for the invocation on hand. It took but ten minutes to make up the required powder. At dinner I laid out my plans to the Captain. He was no longer quite so dismissive of my *heathen mumbo-jumbo*, and agreed to take to his bed within the pentacle to allow my investigation to progress.

"Once more I prepared to stand vigil outside the Captain's room. I sat in the armchair smoking and running the invocation over and over in my head until I was satisfied I had it down pat for if I made even the slightest error both mine and the Captain's very souls could be in danger. I cannot speak the words to you gathered here, for to speak them out of context is also dangerous. Just know my friends that the Sigsand MS was once more about to prove up to the task I had set.

"The air went cold and the shadows grew above the fireplace. A wind whistled in my ears as I rose and slid into the bedchamber. As before, a black shadow grew where there was no light to cast it. Before it had time to press an attack I took the powder from my pocket and, shouting the words of invocation, demanded that the *haunt* reveal itself.

"Frost ran over the windows like a web cast by a crazed spider. The shadow swelled, sending out smoky tendrils. I threw the powder into the air over it.

"The effect was immediate. The shadow fell in on itself and thickened. The air in the room got colder still and ice crackled in my moustache.

"I saw the spear first, the shadow taking form at the blade first, then thickening further to show the wood of the haft. It was then I got my first surprise. I had expected the attacker to be a Zulu warrior from that long-past battle, but the shadow gathered to show a white hand around the spear.

"It thrust the weapon forward towards the bed, but the pentacle held.

"A human form appeared from the shadow. It wore the red-serge uniform of a British soldier. The face showed the grey pallor of death and the eyes were little more than black pools sunk deep in the skull. But there was no mistaking the malice with which the spectre thrust the spear towards the bed.

"Sparks flew throughout the room as the pentacle blazed. Yet it held, even as the attack intensified.

"I was at a loss as to my next move. The Captain decided matters for me. He woke, sitting up in the bed with a jolt and a scream. His gaze fell on the uniformed figure, and puzzlement replaced terror on his face.

"'McKay? Is that you?'

"The spectre showed no sign of hearing him. It continued to press its attack, again and again. The valves of the electric pentacle were beginning to dim and I realized that the battery was being used up rapidly by the efforts needed to repel the attack. Indeed, just as I noticed this, the azure glare faded.

The next thrust of the spear went clean through the protection and took the Captain in the muscle of his right arm. Blood spread quickly through the man's night-shirt and he fell back on the bed.

"As if satisfied, the spectre dissipated. The last thing to go was the spear's tip, red and dripping with the Captain's blood."

Carnacki paused in his telling to allow us a chance to recharge our glasses.

Now that I knew he was injured I could see that he favoured his right hand side, and that there was some stiffness in his bearing that was not usually apparent.

It did nothing to affect his storytelling ability. As usual his tale demanded our full attention.

"Now, gentlemen, we get to the nub of the matter," he said, and we were immediately back into the story.

"Once again I had to rouse the housekeeper to have her perform nursing duties. Afterwards the Captain and I went through to the parlour and started to make inroads in his whisky. I waited until he was on his second glass before broaching the subject at hand.

"'You recognized the man,' I said. It was not a question.

"He stared at the spear, and the new blood there. He was quiet for a while before replying.

"'I have not yet told you the whole story of what occurred at Uluni in seventy-nine, for I did not think it pertinent. Now I am not so sure.

"'McKay and I had fought side by side across three continents and twelve years even before the Zulu war. No man ever had a truer friend, or a more entertaining drinking partner. Uluni proved to be one of the closest scrapes we ever got ourselves in.

"'I have already spoken of the wound I took to my thigh. What I did not tell you is that in taking the wound I was struck from my horse. Two Zulu loomed over me and I made my peace with the Lord, for I thought for sure that my number had come up.

"'McKay had other ideas. He put himself in front of the Zulu and took both of them on, giving me time to remount. He killed both, but took a sore wound in the belly.

"'I carried him from the field myself.'

"He stopped and took a long gulp of the whisky.

"'The wound suppurated in the infernal heat. McKay was sent back home to a sanatorium and was years in healing. Even then, he was never the same man again. We kept in touch for a while, but it is more than twenty years since I have seen or heard of him.

"'Until tonight.'

"He finished his whisky and headed for the bottle.

"'What did we see?' he whispered. 'Did we see a ghost?'

"'I believe so. And a malevolent one at that.'

"Little more was said that night. The Captain turned the conversation to more mundane matters. I could see that he had taken a sore fright, and I respected his desire for some distance from the earlier events. We talked of politics and cricket until the whisky was gone and this sunlight filtered in from outside. Only then did the Captain feel safe in retiring to bed. I left him to sleep and ventured out into the city in search of answers."

"I have never underestimated the power of legwork and money in getting to the bottom of matters, and both proved worthy that same morning.

"The housekeeper had not heard of the man McKay – the Captain had never told her the tale. She did however know much of the ways of the city, and was able to direct me to places the good Captain would never suspect existed.

"Noon found me in a bar in the waterfront area of Leith full of old salts and old soldiers all attempting to lose themselves in liquor. It was the third such place I had visited, and my wallet was far emptier that it had been previously. But I had the scent of the hunt in my nostrils. I was closing in on my man.

"My instincts were proven right. It took half an hour and three different conversations, but I left the bar with an address and a picture in my mind of an old soldier brought low first by sickness then by envy."

"The address proved to be little more than a hovel, and the men that lived there had sunk as low as one can get without disappearing from the face of the earth completely. Every man stank of cheap liquor, and none had seen a washhouse in many months. It was here that I finally found the last piece of the puzzle. A decrepit figure with more fingers than teeth told how McKay had taken to begging on the streets of the city to pay for liquor. One day, in the Castlegate, he had approached a military man, only to be instantly rebuffed.

"The recognition had only been one way. McKay had seen the man whose life he had saved. The Captain had seen just another beggar.

"The last months of McKay's life had been full of bitterness and envy, and he had gone to his grave several weeks past cursing Captain McLeod, and vowing that he would have his day, in this life or the next.

"It seems the latter was to be the case."

Carnacki paused to refill his pipe.

"It was here that I made a near fatal error of judgement. I must ask you, my friends, to forgive this lapse, but having heard my tale, I am sure that you too would have come to the same conclusions as I.

"Indeed, the Captain seemed to find my explanation most probable."

"The Captain's housekeeper plied me with jam tarts as sweet as honey as I laid out my plan for the coming night. I had the Captain send for a battery for the pentacle while I once again made good the defensive barriers. It seems that the Captain had some clout in the town, for the new battery arrived within the hour and I was able to connect the valves just as night started to fall.

"I sat in the armchair reviewing an exorcism from the Sigsand MS which purported to be efficacious in removing a jealous haunt. By the time it got too dim to read I had the spell firmly in my mind and I felt ready, indeed eager, for the night's activities to begin.

"Once again the house fell dark and quiet around me. By now I well knew what to expect, and I had stood and slid into the Captain's room almost as soon as the shadows started to gather above the mantel.

"The Captain had eschewed any thought of sleep. He sat, fully clothed, on the edge of the bed, watching the dark shadows gather outside the softly glowing pentacle. I threw the last of the powder from my pocket over the shade, and pronounced the invocation of revelation I had used the night before.

"Ice ran and crackled in thin tendrils all over the walls. The shadow contracted, darkening and thickening. The air got so cold that each breath felt like it might freeze my very lungs in place.

"The spear took form first and the shadow gathered to once more show the thin white hand around the haft as the weapon was thrust forward towards the bed.

"The pentacle blazed. Sparks flew, but the defences held.

"McKay's form appeared from the shadow, the red-serge uniform the colour of fresh blood. He raised the spear for another blow. Fearing that the battery might not survive a further series of attacks, I stepped forward and called out the exorcism. As I spoke McKay's dead black eyes stared straight at me, and the cold seemed to pierce my very soul. But he held his attack as my badly-spoken Latin rang around the room.

"The spell came to an end.

"*ADJÚRO ergo te, omnis immundíssime spíritus, omne phantásma, omnis incúrsio sátanæ, in nómini Jesu Christ.*

"My declamatory shouting had been to no avail. McKay's form did not fade. Indeed the cold seemed to deepen further, and the spectre took on an even closer semblance of life.

"It continued to press the attack and once more the pentacle blazed with sparks. McKay was more solid now, and I had a clear view of both the spear and the red serge uniform. A gaping wound showed where the man had taken a stab to the guts. Blood dripped, thick heavy drops vanishing before they hit the floor.

"I shouted the last line of the chant again.

"*ADJÚRO ergo te, omnis immundíssime spíritus, omne phantásma, omnis incúrsio sátanæ, in nómini Jesu Christ.*

"Once more the attack continued unabated. Even the new

battery was not going to take much more. The blue glare was already less bright. McKay lunged forward with the spear aimed straight at the Captain's heart. The old soldier threw himself to one side just in time.

"As McKay withdrew from the thrust I immediately realized that I had made a mistake in my judgement. The weapon that pressed the attack was not the same as the one over the mantel, being several feet longer and with a much thinner blade. And as McKay's form grew more distinct, I saw a phantom outline of the Iklwa, stuck in its place, deep in the wound in his belly!

"I ran out into the parlour as if the dogs of hell were at my heels.

"The Iklwa was where I expected, above the mantel. Fresh blood dripped from the blade. And now I knew the truth of it. The blood was neither the Captain's, nor mine, but McKay's, from the wound in his gut.

"I pulled the weapon from its moorings on the wall with some force, taking some of the paint and plaster with it. Once again at a run I made for the Captain's bedchamber, arriving just in time to see the thrusting spear pierce the old man in the left shoulder.

"The valves of the pentacle were almost spent. At any moment the defences would fail completely, and the old man would surely be killed. I hefted the iklwa and stepped into the circle, putting myself between McKay and the old man.

"The focus of the attack immediately switched to me, and I found myself in a fight for my life. The iklwa clashed with McKay's assagai. More sparks flew -- the last remnants of the protection. The blue glow surged brightly for a second as the battery had one last hurrah. Then the defences were gone.

"The spectre lunged forward in a blow that would have

pierced my heart if I had not seen it coming. I stepped inside it – and thrust the iklwa deep into McKay's gut. The material weapon in my hand merged with the immaterial already lodged in the man's belly. The spectre howled -- a wail of anguish and pain I will hear for many nights to come.

"The weapon in my hands went as cold as a stone in a winter river as McKay fell apart into black shadows. The darkness thrashed violently and loomed over me, reaching for the Captain. The iklwa seemed to leap in my hands. It stabbed into the shadow. The blackness immediately fell apart, like burnt paper turning to ash in a wind.

"A cold breeze blew through the room. Suddenly the night had fallen quiet. I let the weapon fall to the floor and followed it down to the ground where I sat on my haunches, totally spent."

"In the morning we buried the iklwa in the Captain's garden. The old man said the words and sang *Onward Christian Soldiers.* Then we returned to the parlour and made strong inroads into another bottle of his fine Scotch, each of us trying not to look at the blank space above the mantle.

"We both needed several days to recover from our wounds, in which time we made a nuisance of ourselves with the housekeeper. Each day I rebuilt the defences in the pentacle, but they were not required.

"The old man was distraught to think that he might have caused at least some of his own woes by being less than charitable to an old comrade in arms.

"'Was he brought here by the iklwa – or by his rage at me?' he said.

"I could not give him a straight answer. In my heart I believe that McKay and the spear were joined together in an unholy matrimony, even as far back as the time of the original wounding.

"Only one thing is clear.

"The iklwa, and the man it had ultimately killed, are now both at rest."

Carnacki was solemn as he showed us out.

"Out you go," he said, but without his usual smile. Indeed none of us felt much like talking and we left, each man making his own way along the Embankment in silence.

It was to be several weeks before another card came inviting us to 427, Cheyne Walk and in truth, I was glad of the break.

The Larkhill Barrow

Carnacki's card of invitation arrived just as I was starting to wonder what he was up to *this* time. On Friday evening I arrived at seven o' clock prompt at his lodgings in Chelsea at 427, Cheyne Walk.

Carnacki motioned me through to the parlour where I found the three others already there awaiting me. It was not long before Carnacki, Arkwright, Jessop, Taylor and I were all seated at Carnacki's dining table. As usual talk was confined to inconsequential gossip until we repaired to the parlour for after-dinner drinks. By the time we got our glasses filled and our smokes lit we were all on tenterhooks, eager for the tale of Carnacki's latest escapades.

He did not keep us waiting, launching straight into a story that immediately had us captivated.

"I am sorry it has been so long since our last meeting," he began. "But I have been under a veil of secrecy that has only today been lifted. The reason for all the cloak and dagger flummery will become apparent as my tale unfolds, but let me begin by assuring you that it is as strange a story as any I have ever related, made stranger still for being performed under the auspices of His Majesty's Royal Artillery.

"It began some three weeks ago with a telegram.

"'Request your services immediately at Larkhill Barracks. George Blandford (Colonel)'

"Now you chaps know me by now. I am not the kind of man to turn down such a request, no matter how curtly it has presented itself. The next morning I was on a train to Salisbury and from there by cab to the testing ground at Larkhill.

"I was almost turned away at the perimeter by an over officious guardsman, but once I showed him the telegram I was allowed through and was escorted by an armed soldier to a tented village. There, in the largest of the tents, I was finally presented to Colonel Blandford.

"It was immediately apparent that the man was in quite a funk. Indeed, he seemed less like a military man and more like someone on the verge of diving into a bottle with no intent of surfacing. After no more than the most basic of introductions he launched into his story. As he talked, it was punctuated by munitions going off all around us, and that only served to lend verisimilitude to the yarn he spun.

"'Before I start,' he said. 'I must inform you that this must remain strictly confidential. If word of what is happening here ever gets out, it may give the enemy a distinct advantage.'

"I did not bother inquiring as to *which* enemy. There is always one.

"The Colonel continued.

"'It began last week. We were ordered to start testing on a new gun, the Hotchkiss Mark I. We had it set up on a mound out on the plain that we have used in the past as a piece of higher ground. Gunnery Sergeant Rogers was keen to see what the new weapon could do and once we had the dummies in place he set about mowing them down, thirty rounds at a time. The air was full of the din for many seconds.

"'I went to inspect the damage to the dummies, but only got halfway across the field when Sergeant Rogers started to scream. Now you must understand Mr. Carnacki. Rogers is one of the stoutest men I have ever served alongside. Yet he was in such terror that he had to be restrained forcefully to prevent injury to himself.

"'A few stiffeners in the mess later and he was more his old self again, but no amount of ordering was going to get him back on that mound. He has not talked of exactly *what* brought on such terror, but that night everyone in camp got a small taste of it.

"The Colonel opened his desk drawer and removed a hip flask. He took a long smooth gulp.

"'It is the nightmares that do it, Mr. Carnacki. Such dreams as no Christian man should have to suffer. Every time we fired that blasted gun on top of the mound the man on the gun suffered a blue funk. The night afterwards, the dreams returned to us all. And the drums -- the infernal drums.

"'After a while we stopped using the mound altogether. We could not get a man to go up there, even under threat of court-martial. But it was too late. The drums, and the dreams have continued for us all.'

"His voice dropped to a whisper.

"'And they are getting stronger.'

"Now I have seen hysteria before now," Carnacki continued. "But never among a band of military men hardened by battle and united in camaraderie. At that stage I thought they might be suffering from a common delusion, but I would not know the details of the matter until I got to the cause.

"That afternoon I went out onto the firing range with a young private who was clearly terrified even before we got close to the mound.

"'You do not have to do this,' I said to him as we left the Colonel's tent.

"He was ashen-faced and his lower lip trembled. He looked to be no more than eighteen years old and his uniform had clearly been intended for a larger man. But his gaze was clear and bright as he looked me in the eye.

"'I have my orders sir,' he replied. "And Jimmy Carruthers ain't no coward.'

"He led me out onto the range.

"Almost immediately I saw the *mound* I realized what it was. It was a long barrow, a large example of the species that are found liberally scattered all over the Plain and surrounding hills. Remarkably this one seemed to be still intact, having never been plundered by treasure seekers.

"I was soon to find that there was a good reason that this particular site had remained unspoiled.

"Even before we started to make our way up the slight incline I felt the malign influence of the place. It *thrummed*, like a dynamo underfoot, and the young private stopped, unsure as to what he was feeling.

"I put a hand on his shoulder.

"'I am here with you lad. Let us get this over with, then you and I can have a smoke and a beer in the mess.'

"He smiled at that, and it was enough to get him moving, but by Jove, we wanted to turn and flee with every step. The view from the top of the mound temporarily relieved the symptoms. We looked out from a raised elevation over a large flat plain. Some five hundred yards distant stood a row of straw dummies – our target for the test.

"The Hotchkiss gun lay under a tarpaulin and it was a matter of seconds before Carruthers was ready. He lay on his belly and set aim at the dummies. I pressed my hands over my ears, but the din when he started to fire was still deafening.

"Now you chaps know that I have faced terror many times afore now, and have been so close to death that I have felt its cold breath on my face. But those times were all as nothing compared to the sheer funk that descended on me as those shots were fired and the mound began to echo in time.

"It began with a reverberating vibration that shook the ground beneath us, as if a giant might be attempting an awakening from a buried sleep. Carruthers tried to stand but the shaking was so violent that he immediately fell back to lie on the ground beside the gun, fear huge in his eyes. The vibrations soon shook me to my very core, threatening to shake my flesh loose from my bones. I too fell on the grassy mound as darkness seeped in at the edge of my sight.

"In less time than it took to draw a breath I was blinded, groping in the darkness as the ground rose and fell around us.

"But that was not the worst of it. I was in blackness. But I was not alone.

"A drumbeat had started and I felt it just as much in the pit of my stomach as I heard it in my ears – a giant drum, distantly far, but getting closer every second, beating as fast as my terrorized heart. Something moved in the dark, something huge. I was lost in a world of fear, like a child in a dark room when he senses movement under his bed. The blackness surged, washing over me in waves. I wished I were dead so that I might be free of this. Somewhere in the dark young Carruthers screamed, but try as I might I was unable to find him. I was utterly lost, utterly alone.

"And just as I thought I could take no more, something in the blackness reached for me."

Carnacki paused to knock the ash from his pipe and refill it from his tobacco pouch. None of us spoke. We knew from long experience not to disturb the flow of the story at this juncture. There would be plenty of time for questions later – if any were needed.

"It was not *my* fortitude, but that of young Carruthers that saved us from any assault. By some means he got his hands in the weapon and fired round after round into the ground at our feet. My sight recovered sufficiently to see mud and earth fly where the shots tore into the ground. The giant drumbeat faltered. It did not stop completely, but its effects diminished sufficiently that I was able to drag the young soldier off the mound and onto safer ground.

"The further we got from the source, the more the feelings receded until we were able to drop to the ground, ourselves once more, but totally spent.

"And that is where the Colonel and the others found us, lying a hundred yards from the mound and too weak to stand, too weak even to speak. I was ignominiously carried off to a tent and a camp bed that felt better than any feather pillow.

"Sleep did not come easily. Every time I closed my eyes I saw blackness where something dark, huge and *old* lurked. I didn't know whether it was aware of me or not, but I did not wish to take any chances. My whole body seemed to sing with a deep bass note that took hours to subside and even then I still felt it when I touched my teeth with my tongue. I could lie there no longer. I got up and went in search of a smoke.

"As always, a pipe of my best shag soon had me calm and able to consider the situation with some degree of rationality. Soon I had convinced myself. I believed the origin of the happenings to lie in a strange but perfectly understandable cause that I have seen before, and indeed, I have previously related the story to you chaps. You may remember my tale of the Jarvee and the phenomenon known as attractive vibrations. Harzam, in his monograph on "Induced Hauntings," points out that such are invariably produced by "induced vibrations," that is, by temporary vibrations set up by some outside cause. Well I had my cause, in the rhythmic *rat-a-tat* of the gunfire. Something in the mound was *sympathetic* to the sound, and answering in kind.

"All I had to do was prove it, and for that, I was going to need both the help of the Colonel, and the use of some equipment I had at hand back in my lodgings in London.

"Before repairing back to the camp bed I told the Colonel of my plans, and had him send for my things. I retired to bed happy that I had taken some degree of control over the situation.

"That feeling lasted only as long as it took me to fall asleep. The dream came immediately.

"It started in pitch blackness. A drum was beat in the distance, a deep thudding like a hammer on metal. I tried to wake myself, for somehow I knew this to be a dream, but I was locked in place, unable to move, unable even to scream as the beat grew louder and the blackness darkened. Soon the drum pounded in my ears so loud that I thought I would never hear anything else again. In the dark something shifted… and moved closer.

"I woke in a cold sweat.

"I immediately knew that there would be no more sleep for me that night. I took my pipe and went outside. As I lit up I could see thin tendrils of smoke drifting skywards from tents all around me. Lamps were on in many of them and I could hear murmured conversations from the bigger tents where several men were billeted together. I doubt if there was a single man in the camp yet asleep.

"In the morning the Colonel took my advice and raised camp, moving the whole operation several miles to the north. It took until well after noon, but it was immediately apparent that the moral of the troops had improved.

"As for myself, I approached the mound with some trepidation, but I was determined to prove my theory of *induced vibrations*.

"To my surprise and delight young Carruthers volunteered to accompany me. I also prevailed on the Colonel for the assistance of a draftsman. This turned out to be a serious chap from Yorkshire by the name of Brown who scarcely uttered a word but produced the most wonderful detailed drawings.

"We spent much of that first day in measuring and describing the exterior dimensions of the mound. There was no repeat of the terrors of the day before, although there *was* a constant low thrumming all across the mound, as if something was just waiting to be kicked into action once more.

"Carruthers and myself left Brown to finish his preliminary drawing and lit up some smokes. The young private was obviously already an old hand. He had rolled a needle-thin smoke and had it lit even before I got my pipe full. He held it cupped backwards in his hand to protect it from the wind and when he took a drag of smoke it was the furtiveness of a man well used to taking his pleasure under the threat of being found out.

"We were still smoking when Brown called us over. His examination of the ground had borne fruit and he stood in a slight depression. He had pulled some of the topsoil aside and pointed downward to a deeper hole that led into blackness.

"We had found the entrance.

Carnacki paused once more -- this time to allow us to recharge our glasses and get some fresh smokes going. While we were occupied he himself sat and stared into the fire. I noticed for the first time that there were dark bags under his eyes, and a strain showing there that I had never previously seen.

He looked like a man who had not slept well for quite some time. Indeed, I would have prevailed on him to save the tale for another night, but he waved me aside, intent on continuing.

"I went down into the barrow later that afternoon armed with nothing more than a lamp. At first the interior looked as I would have expected. The walls were built of large blocks of sandstone, beautifully engineered and dovetailed together so tight that you could scarce slip a sheet of paper between them. I have visited several Neolithic tombs, in Carnac, in Orkney and on Dartmoor. This gave the same sense of age, of a time long past. What I hadn't expected, what was completely different, was the overwhelming feeling that this place was in use.

"The initial chamber was some ten feet long, and half as

wide. Small passages led off on either side leading to sub-chambers, all of which were dry, but empty. Brown entered behind me and started to make measurements. Young Carruthers loitered at the entrance, too scared to enter, but driven by his duty to help me. I took pity on him and told him he could have a smoke break as I headed deeper into the mound.

"The ground descended at the far end of the chamber, leading me down an incline and into a larger room beyond.

"It was a rough-hewn chamber of some antiquity, and unlike the smaller chambers near the entrance, this one was far from empty. The walls were covered in small, tightly packed carvings. At first I thought it might be a language, but it was none that I recognized from my studies, indeed, it seemed to bear no resemblance to anything I had ever seen before. Brown was equally as puzzled when he arrived and the pair of us spent some time studying all the carvings searching for meaning. None came.

"All the time I had been in the mound I was aware that the vibrations underfoot continued apace. But as yet there was no sign of any drumming or anything that might suggest a return to the full shaking terrors of the day before.

"For that, I needed the trigger, but I was loath to implement that plan without a better understanding of the outcome. That meant there was nothing for it but to try and decipher the carvings. Brown and I started in straight away, him taking meticulous drawings as I divided the large wall area into manageable sectors.

"Light was fading on the first day before we emerged and dragged our weary bodies across to the camp's new location. That night everyone slept soundly, with no interruptions for dark things moving to the beat of giant drums.

"Morale in the camp was much improved in the morning, and my own spirits were raised by the arrival of my things from London, including the two phonographs I had requested."

Carnacki had not paused, but Jessop interrupted the tale.

"Phonographs? Oh, I say. Have you got the four-minute cylinders? They say the quality is the best yet, although Gramophone quality is also improving. I believe discs are going to be the thing to have next year. But..."

If allowed, Jessop would go on about his equipment for hours. Luckily one look from Carnacki put paid to *that*.

Carnacki allowed us a second to settle before resuming.

"We spent the next three days merely cataloguing the extent of the wall carvings in the chamber, and poor Brown was exhausted by the end of it. But he had provided me with a complete annotation of everything we could see. Unfortunately I could still make neither head nor tail of it. The Sigsand MS was no help, holding no descriptions of any such markings. I saw nothing for it but to proceed with the experiment and pull the trigger.

"The case took on a further degree of urgency when the men sleeping nearest the mound started to complain of a return of the dreams. It seemed the effects of the mound were still spreading.

"The next morning Carruthers helped me record the sound of the Hotchkiss Mark I onto a cylinder. Then we lugged the phonograms and a battery big enough to drive them down to the mound.

"Once again I took pity on the lad and allowed him to stay at the entrance as I went down to the chamber. We had set the two phonograms in the centre of the space. I steeled myself for whatever might happen and set the first cylinder going.

"The sound of gunfire filled the chamber.

"The drumming started almost immediately. I set the second phonogram to record and left the chamber at a run. Even before I reached the entrance I could feel the darkness creep and reach for me. I threw myself out into the open just as it threatened to blind me. Carruthers half-carried me across the Plain until we reached a place where the vibrations were manageable and we stood, sharing one of his smokes. After what seemed like an age the drumming finally subsided. I crept back into the mound and retrieved the phonographs.

"I had my recording. But it had come at a cost. That same night the dreams came again, to every man in the camp."

"Matters did not improve in the morning. I was summoned to the Colonel's tent to be met by an officious little man in a suit who was introduced as *Jenkins from the Ministry*.

"This man proved to be most interested in my research, and indeed seemed to know every detail of what had already occurred. He demanded to listen to the recording I had made the day before. I tried to appeal to the Colonel, but it seemed that the *Ministry* man outranked anyone else at the camp. Even when I explained what I considered to be the danger of sympathetic vibrations, still the man insisted. I had no choice but to comply.

"I had no idea what the outcome would be of playing the recording. The trigger, I already knew, was the rhythm of the gunfire, but I also knew from a harsh lesson learned that the very sound of the drumming would induce terror in even the strongest of hearts while in the vicinity of the mound.

Whether that would be the case here in the camp, I had no way of knowing. It was with some trepidation that I switched on the phonogram.

"The sound of drumming filled the tent and I waited for a reaction.

"The syncopated rhythm might have set one's feet tapping, but the drumming proceeded to its end with no other power than that.

"I breathed a sigh of relief. The man from the *Ministry* could not conceal his disappointment. After he had left the Colonel explained the situation.

"'The *Ministry* thinks you might have discovered a new weapon. They were hoping to be able to take your cylinder and duplicate it. Just think what would be the outcome if they could take the terror, the nightmares, and induce them in our enemies. We would strike fear into their hearts even before a shot was fired. Think of it.'

"I did indeed think of it. It filled me with almost as much fear as the blackness itself. Even as I lay abed that night I could think of little else. And when sleep did finally come, it was filled with my worst nightmare, a creeping blackness inching ever closer, reaching -- always reaching.

"I woke covered in a cold clammy sweat to find that less than ten minutes had passed. But there would be no more sleep that night.

"In the morning I set to the task of deciphering the markings, for I now believed that they held the secret to halting the nightly assault on our senses."

Carnacki stopped and set about refilling his pipe. I noticed that his movements were slow and deliberate, as if he needed to concentrate fully on the task. I saved him a journey and refilled his whisky glass.

In the lull, Jessop tried to apologize for his earlier gaffe, but Carnacki waved him away with a tired smile.

"I will be happy to hear your views on the latest recording techniques," he said. "For they will be most useful in future investigations. But for now, let me finish this tale, for I find myself growing tired, and I would like to end tonight if I can."

We all recharged our glasses for the last time and lit up our smokes to add to the growing fug in the parlour.

"For three more days Brown and I knocked our heads against the enigma that was the markings. I must have pored over his drawings a hundred times, and listened to the wax cylinder as many times again.

"The nights were the worst, filled with the screams of those who were able to sleep, and the constant grumbling of those who struggled to stay awake. I smoked twice as much as usual and each morning arose with a mouth tasting of ash and a pounding headache.

"On the fourth morning news started to filter in of disturbances in the night in surrounding towns. The effect was spreading.

"Orders came down from on high that the situation had to be dealt with immediately, but neither the Colonel or I had any idea how to comply with such a request. It was when the Colonel informed me that he intended to pack the mound with explosives and *send it to hell where it belongs* that I decided drastic action of a different kind was required.

"Carruthers came with me down to the mound, the pair of us lugging the phonographs and battery between us. This time the young man insisted on standing with me in the chamber as I switched on both recordings simultaneously. The sound of gunfire echoed and joined with the drumming. The chamber rang and echoed, a cacophonous din assaulting our ears. The shaking also came almost immediately, first through the soles of my feet then up my spine until my very skull rattled and hummed. My sight started to go soon after than, blackness creeping until I was once more totally blind.

"Every part of me screamed that I should run, but I stood my ground. I felt young Carruther's cold hand in my palm. The drumming thudded through me, sending my stomach seething and roiling. The blackness thickened and again I felt *something* move.

"Still I stood my ground. The noise was almost unbearable.

"The *thing* kept moving in the darkness. It reached for me.

"And then it happened. The drumming in the room reached a new frenzy. Dust and rubble shook free from the ceiling.

"The blackness receded... slowly at first, then quicker as the drumming reached a crescendo.

"The cylinders played out. The drumbeats echoed in the chamber for a while then died away. The darkness slowly cleared. The first thing I saw was Carruther's pale white face, his eyes staring wildly.

"Still hand in hand we stumbled outside where he voided the contents of his stomach in the grass. I almost felt like joining him, but my mind was working faster than my body.

"I had learned something. The darkness was much more than just a vibration artefact – it was a malevolent entity, intent on breaking through into our world. And the drumming did not *bring* the darkness.

"It kept the darkness at bay.

"By the time my meeting with the Colonel came round in the afternoon I had the beginnings of a thesis.

"Brown provided the missing link barely an hour before the meeting. He arrived at a run to where I sat in my tent preparing my presentation for the Colonel.

"'It is not a language,' he said, brandishing his drawings in front of my face in his left hand and the cylinder of the drumming recordings in his right. 'It is a notation. Almost musical... but definitely rhythmic. Look.'

"He traced out a patch of his drawing with a finger, then drew my attention to an area of the cylinder. The marks on the wax corresponded almost exactly with the marks on the drawing."

"I took both the drawings and the cylinder with me when I met the Colonel. He was still of a mind to pack the mound with munitions and be done with it, but to his credit he heard me out.

"'I now believe I was in error to ascribe the situation to sympathetic vibrations,' I began.

"That got me a raised eyebrow and a wry smile, but he was enough of a brick about it to allow me to continue.

"'There is indeed an entity residing in the barrow.'

"That got me another raised eyebrow, but I ploughed on regardless.

"'I believe the barrow to be a prison, and the low chamber to be a cage, of sorts. The entity is bound within this chamber by some kind of acoustic bonds, as delineated by the carvings on the walls. We have somehow loosened these bonds by firing the weapon atop the mound, the rhythm of the gun in some manner providing a *key* to the locks that bind the entity. It is obvious that we have given the being a way of partially escaping its cell, and it has taken the opportunity, visiting us nightly in our dreams, and testing the defences for a way to escape completely.'

"The Colonel stopped me in full flow.

"'It may be obvious to you old man,' he said. "But it's dueced odd all around. Are you sure a bomb wouldn't be efficacious?'

"'I am sure,' I said. "To do so would release the bonds completely, and the entity would be free. I suspect we would quickly see just how effective the hoped-for weapon would be. The whole country would be in uproar in days.'

"The colonel went white as a sheet.

"'Can't we just close up the mound and stop using the gun?'

"I shook my head.

"'The *key* has already been turned in the lock.'

"'Then what do you suggest?'

"I trusted my instincts.

"There is a solution I have attempted with some success in the past," I said. "I have it among my things. With your permission, I would like to try destroying the entity completely."

Carnacki stopped and stared into the fire.

"I have been considering how much of the detail of this case I should relate," he said. "I have years of experience of dealing with such matters. But you chaps here have only experienced at second hand the awful powers of beings from the Outer Ring... for that is what I had on my hands down in that chamber. An entity so vast as to be almost incomprehensible, completely without interest in the acts of mere humans, yet with the capacity to destroy us all utterly should we allow it access to this plane. I do not wish to burden you, my friends, with thoughts so dark that they will invade your dreams.

"Yes, the entity was indeed from that same psychic circle as I told of in the tale of Wilton's Hog. I believe it to be a similar kind of thing, something whose existence plagued the builders of the old stones and barrows out there on the Plain. Indeed I believe in some respects that the old stones are aligned in their fashion *because* of the Outer Ring, in an ancient attempt to control and divert the powers in much the same way as I do myself with more modern technology. You get my line of suggestion?"

I am afraid none of us sat in the parlour were quite able to follow his thinking.

Carnacki sighed and sat back in his chair.

"Maybe the means by which I reached a conclusion will make things clearer."

"The next morning I started by inscribing the protective circles on the chamber floor. I began with the basic protections from the Sigsand MS.

"I began by drawing a circle of chalk, using a piece of string anchored to a centre point and taking care never to smudge the line as I navigated my way around the chamber. Beyond this I rubbed a broken garlic clove in a second circle around the first.

"When this was done, I took a small jar of purified water and went round the circle again just inside the line of chalk, leaving a wet trail that dried quickly behind me. Within this inner circle I made my pentacle using the signs of the Saaamaaa Ritual, and joined each Sign most carefully to the edges of the lines I had already made.

46

"In the points of the pentacle I placed five dry biscuits wrapped in linen, and in the valleys five vials of the purified water. Now I had my first protective barrier and with this first stage complete the centre of the chamber, now protected as it was by the most basic of spells, already felt more secure.

"I have told you enough tales by now for you not to need a description of my electric pentacle, for you know that it has saved me many times already, and proves most efficacious against many emanations and disturbances.

"I have made several improvements in recent months, and when I set the mechanism to overlay the drawn pentagram upon the floor and connected up the battery, the glare shone from the intertwining vacuum tubes. You may expect me to tell of the azure glow, but my improvements, coming as they have from long study on the ways of the Outer Circle, have led me to include other colours. The Sigsand manuscript puts it thus:-

Nor can he abide in the Deep if ye adventure against him armed with red purple. So be warned. Neither forget that in blue, which is God's colour in the Heavens, ye have safety.

"My interpretation of this, I must tell you, consists of seven glass vacuum circles -- the red on the outside of the pentacle, and the remainder lying inside it, in the order of orange, yellow, green, blue, indigo and violet.

"Once I was sure that the vacuum valves were all operating correctly, I stood in the centre of the circles and readied the phonographs.

"Just before I started young Carruthers called from the entrance. He, stout lad, had offered to stand beside me once more, but I could not in all conscience expose him to such danger. I had him stand in the upper chamber. The Colonel, as a precaution, had already filled the side chambers with black powder. Carruthers was in charge of the detonator, to be used in the event of my abject failure.

"I called back to the lad, indicating that all was ready, then started up the recording of the gunfire. The effect was immediate. I felt it first through the soles of my feet, but soon my whole frame shook, vibrating in time with the rhythm. My head swam, and it seemed as if the very walls of the chamber melted and ran. The pentacle receded into a great distance until it was little more than a pinpoint of light in a blanket of darkness, and I was alone, in a vast cathedral of emptiness where nothing existed save the dark and the pounding beat.

Shapes moved in the dark, wispy shadows with no substance, shadows that capered and whirled as the drum grew ever more frenetic. I gave myself to it, lost in the dance, lost in the dark.

I know not how long I wandered, there in the space between. I forgot myself, forgot my duty, in blackness where only rhythm mattered. I believed I had been there for an age, but I was brought back directly to the pentacle when the cylinder on the phonograph played itself out. Only two minutes had passed.

"Thankfully I still stood in the centre of the pentacle. A giant drum beat around me, but now that the *key*, the gunfire, had been stopped, I felt no call to join in the blackness.

"Beyond the pentacle, despite the fact that the valves glowed brightly, the chamber was filled with darkness, shadows so deep that I could not see the carved walls. For the first time I could sense my adversary directly, probing at my defences, looking for a passage through. It was time to begin the *expulsion*.

"I replaced the cylinder in the phonograph with one that

Brown and I had worked up. Our markings on the wax matched a passage of rhythm mentioned in the Sigsand MS as being used by certain tribesmen in removing malevolent spirits. I did not yet know whether it would work, but I had no option but to give it a try.

"I also attached my electric pentacle to the phonograph, such that the spectrum of would glow in time with any sound. I started the cylinder spinning more in hope than in any expectation of success.

"The phonograph sounded thin and tinny in comparison to the deep drumming that echoed in the chamber, but when the valves started to flash in time the drums seemed to falter and the darkness thinned enough that I could momentarily see the walls of the chamber. I almost let out a cry of victory, but I was premature.

"The blackness surged. Sparks flew from all the valves, the sudden light so bright I had to squeeze my eyes shut, and even then the afterimage stayed there for long seconds. The defences held, for a while. But I knew I only had mere minutes before the phonograph cylinder would play itself out, leaving me only with the electric pentacle between the entity and myself. From what I had seen, I knew that if I were to wait that long I would be a goner.

"I started to chant in time with the recordings, meaningless sounds in a voice made throaty with fear. But the new sound found some sympathy in the walls of the chamber itself, as if they had been hewn for this very purpose.

"A new beat grew, a bass drum in perfect time with my chanting.

"Once more the darkness threw itself forward against my defences.

"Several of the valves started to dim, and my voice

faltered... just for a fraction of a second. The blackness swelled and pressed an attack stronger than any previously made. The valves flickered and dimmed. I raised my voice, putting more depth into the chant, aware that there were mere seconds left to me.

"In answer the whole chamber seemed to swell in song, my own voice echoed and amplified, as if recorded and re-recorded on a thousand phonographs simultaneously. Even as the valves failed completely the blackness shrunk and diminished. A valve popped and I was forced to blink. When I looked again it was just in time to see the blackness hover over the phonograph, like a black cape falling over the contraption.

"The cylinder played out with a last dying *whirr*. The blackness fell into the drum then was gone. The echoes faded and died and my chant died with them. I stood in a sudden silence."

"I may have been standing there yet if the tremulous voice of young Carruthers had not inquired after my health in a loud voice that had more than a hint of fear in it. When I emerged from the lower chamber he almost set off the detonator in his fright, and I had to prise his hand gently from the handle lest he send us both to the place the Colonel intended for the barrow.

"The Colonel himself was disinclined to believe that the situation was controlled with no evidence to prove it, but that night the whole camp slept peacefully.

"The man from the *Ministry* arrived the next day and demanded from me that I show him how to use and control the *blackness*. I told him the truth. I did not know how.

"I did not however tell him of that last second in the

chamber, and how the darkness had been absorbed into the cylinder.

"And no one but me has seen hide nor hair of that piece of wax.

"Until now."

Carnacki reached down to the side of his chair and brought up a phonograph cylinder. He traced the grooves and scratches in the wax with his finger.

"What a marvellous thing modern technology is. This single cylinder has done the same job as a rock chamber that must have taken many years to hew from the ground.

He showed the cylinder to Jessop and smiled.

"I believe it to be safe, as long as I keep it far from the sound of the Hotchkiss Mark I. What say you Jessop? Would you like to hear what happens when you play this back on your equipment?"

Jessop went white and shook his head.

Later, after Carnacki had shown us out with his usual jaunty *out you go*, Jessop and I walked together along the embankment. He was quiet for a long time, but when he spoke, I knew exactly what he had been thinking.

"You know, I think they are right. I think the *Gramophone* is the way of the future."

The Sisters of Mercy

"I have been pondering just how much, if any, of this story to tell you chaps," Carnacki began after we were all settled in his parlour. "For this is no tale of far off places. This did not happen in Scotland, or on a remote firing range on Salisbury Plain. No, this incident was so close that two of you here present will undoubtedly have walked within a hundred yards of the spot this very night. If I tell you the story, you might never feel safe on the Embankment or its environs again."

He said it with a smile, and, of course, after such a start, none of us were going to let him off the hook. He gave us time to fill our glasses and get smokes going, then he began.

"You will remember that last Sunday was a very foggy day," he said. "A dim yellow glow hung over the river. I had taken a stroll across the bridge and along the south side before returning via Vauxhall Bridge to the north Embankment. The damp air meant that any feeling of well being I might have gained from the walk was lost in the almost overbearing fug and I was looking forward to sitting by the fire here in the parlour.

"Indeed, if it had not been for the fog itself, I would almost have been in sight of home when the figure loomed out of the gloom in front of me. I recoiled at first, fearing an attack before I realized my error. It was a short elderly gentleman, hair wild and eyes staring. He wore nothing more than a pair of white flannel pyjamas. They hung open to the waist, his ribcage showing a rack of bones through almost translucent skin. His feet were bare and filthy, caked with recently trodden mud.

"'Help me sir,' he cried. 'Help me or I'm a goner for sure.'

"He would not look me in the eye, his gaze being aimed at a point in the fog to my right hand side. Before I could even reply to his pleas he had turned and fled.

"I quickly lost sight of him. I turned to follow the line of his gaze. Just at the far limits of what I could see, three dark figures moved quickly to flank me and move in the same direction taken by the old man. Their forms were too vague to make out any detail, but they seemed to be wearing long robes of a sort that hung all the way to the ground and made their motion resemble something travelling on wheels rather than legs.

"The only noise I heard was a strangled scream from the old man, sounding already distant in the fog. Once more all was quiet.

"Now you chaps know my mind. A mystery such as this is all the excuse I need to stick my nose where it does not belong. Besides, I had nothing more to look forward to that afternoon besides a lonely supper by the parlour fire, so I took myself off to the most obvious place from which a man in flannel pyjamas might have strayed.

"When I arrived at the Royal Hospital entrance it was obvious that something was afoot. Orderlies and nurses scurried along the corridors looking into rooms while others needed all of their efforts to calm the residents, the bulk of whom seemed to be in a state of some distress.

"One chap, older and even thinner than the one I had encountered on the Embankment, was determined to make a break for it and had successfully eluded an orderly. I was of half a mind to allow him to escape, but thought better of it and took him gently by the arms as he attempted to pass me in the doorway. He fought, but with no strength in his arms, and fell against me, spent, after mere seconds.

"'Help us,' he whispered as the orderly gently prized him off me. 'Help us, or we shall surely all be dead in a week.'

"His eyes pleaded with me as he was led away along the corridor. Now you chaps can imagine, all of this was as a red rag to a bull. My dander was up, and I had the scent of a mystery to lead me on. I slipped into a side room when the orderlies were all occupied and found myself in a small dormitory of eight beds. Three of the beds were empty, with clean linen neatly tucked in place. Four were occupied with wan tired-looking men of indiscriminate ages, and a fifth was empty, but the bedclothes had been thrown awry in the occupant's haste to leave.

"I thought all the men were asleep, and was about to back out when the nearest raised his head and motioned me over with a feeble wave of his hand. I had to bend close to his face to hear his hoarse whisper.

"'Don't let the Sisters see you,' he said. 'They don't notice you if you keep quiet. You'll be fine as long as they don't notice you.'

"'What do you mean *Sisters*?'

"'The nuns,' he said. 'The ones who started to visit last week.'

"His voice dropped even lower and his eyes were filled with fear as they stared into mine.

"'Auld Nick has sent them to take us away. And there's no stopping them.'

"Then, spent, he lay back on the bed.

"By this time the mystery had my full attention and, by Jove, I was going to get to the bottom of it. I left the old men to their sleep and went in search of someone who could tell me what was going on.

"Instead I found an over officious little woman who called herself *The Matron* and who tried to brush me out of the door as if I was an errant piece of dust.

"'I am here about the missing man,' I said. 'I believe I have just seen him on the Embankment.'

She did not stop leading me towards the entrance. Her grip on my arm was as strong as a dockhand's.

"'Nonsense,' she said in a voice that would brook no argument. If she had a moustache it would have bristled in indignation. 'Old Mr. Jennings is hiding in a closet smoking that foul pipe of his again. He will be in serious trouble when *I* get my hands on him.'

"'I believe his troubles are rather more serious than that…' I started, but she was in no mood for discussion. She showed me to the door.

"I just had time for one last attempt to reach her.

"'I believe I also saw the *Sisters*,' I called, just as she shut the doors on me.

"The doors swung open again, and for a split-second I thought I had gotten through.

"She stared at me, her face full of scorn.

"'Piffle,' she said. 'Haunts and ghoulies. Tales to scare sick old men to an early grave. I will not have *any* of that talk in *my* hospital.'

"The doors closed on me with a *clunk* that smacked of finality."

Carnacki paused to refill his pipe. While he did so, Jessop piped up.

"I do hope this is not one of those tales where the perpetrators are no more than people in silly masks," he said loudly. "I do find those *most* unsatisfactory indeed."

Carnacki smiled as he lit the pipe, but there was little humour in it.

"Did I not already tell you that the tale would give you cause to think twice about a walk on the Embankment? Hear me out, then tell me whether you wish to take the stroll home alone."

With no further pause he launched back into the story.

"Having been shown the door so thoroughly, my enthusiasm for the mystery had waned somewhat, but it still worried me throughout the evening. Even then I may have given up the chase if a headline had not caught my eye in *The Thunderer* over breakfast.

"'Body clad in pyjamas pulled from the Thames at Westminster. Foul play suspected.'

"Ten minutes later I was on my way to the British Library. I needed to gain a foothold sufficient to allow me access, and in order to do that I would need to have plenty of facts at hand.

"I spent most of the morning chasing up details of deaths at the Royal Hospital and was horrified to find that a dozen old soldiers had passed on in the last two weeks alone. The death rate prior to that had been little more than one a month.

Normally death on this scale, even in a hospital, would have been cause for some scandal, but it seemed that the newspapers were more concerned with flooding in Paris than events closer to home. I had a most pleasant lunch of a pint of porter and a pie in the Museum Tavern before returning to my task with renewed vigour.

"The first hour back proved frustrating as I could find no records of any *Sisters* being involved in the history of the hospital. It was only when I delved deeper, back to the time when Wren was having the foundations put in for the chapel, that I found my first inkling of trouble, the first breadcrumb on my trail.

"The chosen site for the hospital was on top of the uncompleted building of a former theological college founded by James the First. The building was used to house prisoners before and during the Civil War and in the later wars against the Dutch. When Wren's team began excavations for the foundations, they immediately ran into trouble.

"Four of the labourers died in strange circumstances and a fifth went mad, screaming of *Thee Systyrs of Mercie*. The situation was only improved when Wren called in a priest to sanctify the area and after that work proceeded apace.

"It was enough information to get back my zeal for the chase and I found what I was looking for half an hour later.

"A rash of suspicious deaths plagued the theological college in the middle of the Seventeenth Century. It was then being used as a prison, and the inmates started to die horrible deaths while contained in locked cells. As was the wont in those days, witchcraft was suspected, and indeed, three nuns were imprisoned and tortured. Their confession is on record to this day at the Library.

"*Dorritye Smythe and Anne Smythe, systyrs to Mother*

Superior Abigall Smythe of Bow now in prison confarsed before the honoured majastrats upon thire exsaminations heare in Chelsea the 16 day of this enstant subtember 1642 that thire systyr mayd them witches and acknowlidge that they ware lead into that dradfull sin of witchcrift by hir meanse: the fores'd Abigale Smythe.

"The above named persons Each & Every one of them affirm before the Grand inquest that the above written evidences are truth and the Systyrs of Mercie throw ourselfes on the mercy of the majastrats.

"Below that were three scratched signatures.

"They were shown no mercy. They were burned at the stake, on the grounds of the theological college, and the ashes were scattered... on the very spot where the cathedral foundations would later be built.

"The final piece of my puzzle fell into place by what I then thought of as mere coincidence. I was waiting at Liverpool Street Station and could not help overhearing the two gentlemen at my side. They were discussing a current, and several weeks standing, problem on the underground system, between Sloane Square and South Kensington... *a problem that had necessitated a large amount of excavation in the region of the Royal Hospital foundations.*"

Jessop interrupted at this point.

"I am surprised you were not aware of that Carnacki. It has been a bally nuisance for weeks now. I had to go by way of Vauxhall and you know what a dashed inconvenience that is. Something should be done. I have a good mind to..."

A stern but kindly look from Carnacki quickly shut Jessop up and allowed the tale to continue.

"I arrived at the hospital on Tuesday morning armed with

my research. I had taken precautions to bypass the *Matron* by making an appointment with the Governor himself. The woman glared at me from the corridor as I went in to the head office and her frown did not melt, even under my best smile.

"The Governor proved more amenable to my approach. He was more than willing to admit that he had a problem beyond his comprehension. He read my notes from the library with some puzzlement.

"'I am at a loss to understand what *can* be done in such a case,' he said as he passed me a rather fine cigar. I spent the time it took to smoke it telling him of some of my exploits, and I referred him to the Ministry of Defence who, I assured him, would vouch for my credentials after the aid I gave them in the case of the Larkhill Barrow. I left the office in mid-morning, having been given clearance to begin an investigation.

"As I left the Matron was standing suspiciously close to the door. I suspect she had been eavesdropping on our conversation, and the look she threw in my direction as I passed would have curdled milk."

"My first port of call was back to the dormitory I had visited on Sunday. The unmade bed had belonged to Jeffries. The police had indeed identified the body pulled out of the river as the poor man. Cause of death had not yet been identified, but the body showed signs of charring at the neck that suggested heat had been an issue.

"I examined his sleeping area closely. There were no signs of foul play around the bed. And the other men in the dormitory had heard nothing, seen nothing, having been wakened only when the window slammed open as Jeffries departed. I checked the area around the window. There were muddy footprints on the ground outside which looked to match the mud I had seen on the man's feet, but there was no sign that anyone other than Jeffries had stood there.

"As I was about to leave the dormitory the old man who had spoken earlier waved me over once more.

"'Don't let the Sisters see you,' he said in a whisper.

I leaned in close.

"'You have seen them?'

The old man nodded.

"'Every night for the last ten and more when I visit the lavatory. Out in the corridor near the chapel. They *float.*'

"He would say no more, and indeed when I looked back from the doorway he was already asleep.

"I was still not convinced that the mystery to be solved was of supernatural origin for, as you chaps know, I have encountered human trickery enough to know that the ingenuity of some men knows no bounds. There was only one thing for it.

"Leather armchairs were scattered at intervals along the walls in the long main corridor. I chose one that was in a patch of shadow and gave me a view of the chapel door, and I settled myself down into a watching brief.

"I did not find it easy. At first the noise of the hospital workings reassured me that I wasn't quite alone, but that soon stilled as the building started to shut down for the night. Darkness deepened. There was no moon to throw light in the dark corners that grew blacker as the night came. My imagination switched itself to overtime, and I jumped at the merest noise.

"Now you chaps know that it is not easy to put me in a blue funk, but sitting there in that long empty corridor knowing that stout men lay in the adjoining rooms terrified for their very souls put a chill up my spine that was hard to eradicate. I lit a pipe and sucking the smoke helped ground me back in a place where I was not jumping at every shadow.

"The blue fug hung in the still air above my head, like a patch of fog transplanted indoors. I slipped into a watchful reverie, eyes on the chapel door but mind wandering, weighing possibilities and probabilities.

"I know not how long I sat like that, but the pipe bowl was cold in my hand when I registered the first movement by the chapel door.

"At first I thought the pipe-smoke had drifted along the corridor. A bluish haze hung around the door. Even as I spotted it the cloud coalesced and thickened. It seemed to flow from the very wood of the door itself and resolved into three distinct figures. I had seen them before, out in the fog on the embankment.

"But here, in the cold of the night, they had solidified into three females clad in nun's habits, cowls pulled forward to hang over their faces. They stood facing each other as if conversing then turned as one... heading towards me. Although they seemed human, they radiated a pale blue haze around them that cast cold shadows all along the corridor and lent an ethereal glow to the proceedings.

"My blood went cold in my veins. They did indeed seem to *float*, phantom feet not quite touching the ground, and once again I had the impression that there might be wheels under those skirts and not human limbs.

"I pressed myself as far down in the armchair as I was able and held my breath. But they were not interested in me. They glided silently past. I caught a glimpse under the cowl of the nearest but saw only a flash of pale white.

"It was only once they had passed me completely that I realized their intent. They were headed directly for the dormitory where I had left the old men sleeping.

"They had reached the room door even before my legs would obey instructions to stand, and by the time I reached the dormitory the three were leaned over the bed of the old man who had warned me of them.

"The man lay, wide awake, eyes staring at his attackers, mouth wide but seemingly unable to form a scream. The leading nun bent over him and reached for his neck. The air filled with the stench of burning flesh and smoke rose from the bed.

"I could take no more. I leapt forward and made a grab at the habit of the nearest nun. Heat flared through me, as if I had just opened an oven door. The nun turned and the cowl fell back from her head.

"There was no face, only a pale oval of white, as smooth as a billiard ball. But yet I knew that she saw me. Her arms reached for me and the heat burst forth. I felt my eyebrows singe. Fingers, like red-hot pokers, grabbed at my neck. The pain was like nothing I have ever felt. I threw myself backward towards the door and felt skin tear from around my throat and blood flow down inside my shirt.

"Even as I fell I saw that I had at least distracted the nuns from their task. A clamour rose in the room as men sat up in their beds and started to scream and shout.

"The three figures drew away, floating backwards out the door. I was near to a dead faint, but the last I saw before blackness took me away was the blue haze being drawn once more back through the thick wooden door into the chapel."

Carnacki paused.

"It is not the first time I have been touched by denizens of the other realms," he said. "But it is the first that they have left such a deep mark on me."

He drew back his collar to show the marks of the burning he had taken, four fingers on each side of the neck and two at the Adam's apple where thumbs would have pressed. The skin looked red, but was obviously healing.

Jessop was keen for a closer inspection of the wounds so the rest of us took the chance to refill our glasses and light up fresh smokes.

Carnacki re-filled his pipe. He was just about to start when Jessop interrupted.

"But what were those blasted nuns doing Carnacki? What manner of beings were they? Were they ghosts?"

Carnacki smiled and waved Jessop back to his seat.

"I was just about to get to that my friend," he said. "But first I must remind you of something I have mentioned afore now. I do not believe in ghosts. Not in the popular conception of them anyway. But I do believe that malignant forces can be produced in times of great emotion and stress. I have related many tales to you chaps, of these forces, and their dwelling place in the Outer Circle. I believe what the inhabitants of the hospital, and myself, saw as nuns, was in actuality a malign vibration. It was borne up from the deeds of Sixteen Forty-Two -- a vibration brought about by the torture and burning of three Smythe sisters which created a Saiitii manifestation. The continuity of thought produced by the sister's deaths created a positive action on the surrounding material that survived intact in the Outer Circle until led back to this plane by the excavations currently underway in the underground system."

Jessop seemed about to leap in with another question, but

Carnacki was too old a hand to allow the story to be disrupted in this manner.

"The Addenda to Harzan's Monograph on Astral Coordination and Interference explains it all far better than I can," he said. "And I know you all have a copy of your own that you can peruse at your leisure later."

Carnacki settled back in his chair and we knew it was time to get back to his tale. Indeed, we were most impatient to learn what next occurred. He did not keep us waiting.

"I woke out of a stupor to find two pale faces looming over me. At first I thought the nuns were still there and I'm afraid a funk took me such that I had to be held down to prevent further injury. As soon as I was full awake, I was myself once more, and looked up into the face of the old man from the dormitory, and the *Matron*. The old man at least was pleased to see that I was alive.

"I tried to sit up but the *Matron* proved to be an immovable object, holding me down until she had inspected my burns to her satisfaction.

"'You'll live,' she said, and dismissed me into the hands of the old man. I was finally able to sit up, realising as I did so that I had been put in the bed previously occupied by the dead man Jeffries. Early morning sun was coming in through the window behind the bed. I had been out for most of the night.

"The old man watched me carefully as I stood, shakily at first then more confidently. He held out a hand for me to shake.

"'I owe you my life sir,' he said. 'Anything I can do for you, just name it.'

"I left him with my word that I would indeed call on him

if required, and went outside into the corridor for a smoke. I sat back in the same armchair as before and studied the chapel door.

"It was an unremarkable piece of heavy oak, giving no hint of the splendour Wren had wrought on the other side. But it was not the majesty of human achievement that concerned me today. Once I had finished the pipe I made sure the *Matron* was not about and slipped into the chapel."

"I had been inside on several occasions in the past, but always when it was full for a service. At those times it always felt a warm and comforting place to ponder the mysteries, but today, on a chill morning, and knowing of the *entities* that had emanated from here just the previous night, I felt a cold tingle in my spine.

"There was no sign of any disturbance in the chapel itself, but then I had not expected to find any. I went to the rear of the altar and found the stairwell I knew to be there. On a previous visit I had taken these stairs up into the dome. But today I was bound in the opposite direction. I headed down the narrow passage, aware that the cold was deepening with every step.

"I arrived in a low-ceilinged cellar that ran the full length and breadth of the chapel above, the roof being supported by sturdy stone columns set at regular intervals among the large flagstones of the floor. Some light filtered from a low window in the far corner, high on the wall and surely at ground level on the outside.

"There was no sign of movement, but my fingertips tingled, as if in the presence of a charging dynamo. A rumble came from my left and I felt a deeper vibration in the floor – the result no doubt of the continuing excavations in the underground system. Dirt and sand fell into my hair from the ceiling and a vortex of fine dust ran across the cellar floor. I nearly did not spot it, but over in the centre of the cellar a blue haze rose in the air then, as the rumbling receded, disappeared just as quickly.

"I had found the source. Now I needed a plan of action."

Once more Carnacki paused.

"Before I go further, I must tell you of a new avenue of experimentation I have been pursuing these several months. Ever since that affair at the Larkhill Barrow I have been aware that the valves on the electric pentacle draw too much power for them to be efficiently operated from batteries, especially when the *manifestation* is a being of some energy itself.

"I have been testing a cage designed on principles set out by Michael Faraday. You may well know that all electricity goes up to the free surface of a body without diffusing in the interior substance. If a cage can be built of suitable conducting material then no electric field can exist within the cage itself. Now you can see that, given the Outer Circle beings are effectively electric beings, such a cage would prove most efficacious in defending against them.

"All of that is by way of preamble. I had been given to understand by the Governor of the hospital that on no account was I to deploy any psychic defences that might be construed as smacking of *occult mumbo jumbo* within the chapel. I was not going to be able to utilize my usual pentagrammic protections, so I had no choice but to field-test my cage. I have named it a Garder Cage in honour of my good friend who has given me so much help in its construction.

"Now gentlemen, fill up your glasses and replenish your pipes, for we get to the meat of this tale."

We did as requested, and minutes later were once again settled comfortably and awaiting the story's conclusion.

"I had to call on the aid of the Smithkins brothers to help me lug the cage down into the cellar under the chapel," Carnacki began. "And due to the need to keep the operation as quiet as possible, we waited until early evening before carrying out the task. By the time I had everything set up to my satisfaction darkness was starting to fall outside. I paid off the brothers and they left with alacrity, neither wishing to be down in that darkening cellar after nightfall.

"Soon even the light from the small window was gone. I stood in the darkness, shut inside my fine-mesh cage. The only sound was the whispering hum of the current running through the structure. As my eyes adjusted to the dimming light I could also see a faint glow from the controls I had fitted in the door of the cage to allow me to adjust the voltages and strength of the external field.

"Without the use of the pentacle I was at somewhat of a loss as to how I would accomplish the banishment of the entities once they made their appearance, but as long as my defence held I would have time to try several approaches to the matter.

"In that early part of the night it seemed that the only danger I was under was of giving in to boredom. I had run through various incantations from the Sigsand MS in my mind, readying them against the eventuality of needing them. After I was sure I had them down pat I amused myself by playing word games in my mind, but any glamour that had for me quickly faded, and I soon found myself longing for a pipe and some fine single malt.

"After two more hours of this I was close to giving up for

the night. And, as is usual, that is when the action started.

"Once more it began with a distant rumble. Fine dust pattered down from above and sparks flew where it hit the roof of the cage. Some four feet to my left a luminous blue haze rose from the floor and started to drift upwards, growing as it came up out of the flagstones. It moved quickly towards the ceiling of the cellar and I quickly realized that it intended to head up to the chapel and hence back to the dormitory of sleeping men.

"I turned up the voltage and the humming sounded louder in my ears.

"The blue haze coalesced into three figures, indistinct at first, then solidifying into the pale blue nuns I had seen the night before. Three blank faces, too white in the dim light, turned and stared at my cage. I suddenly remembered the old man's words.

"'*Don't let the Sisters see you,*' he had said. '*They don't notice you if you keep quiet. You'll be fine as long as they don't notice you.*'

"It was rather too late for that.

"At least I seemed to be safe for the time being. The nuns floated silently through the cellar, circling the cage as if confused by its very presence in their domain. After a period of contemplation they positioned themselves, one on either side of me and one directly in front.

"I intended to experiment with the effect of increasing and decreasing the strength of the field around the cage, but I wasn't given the time. As one, they launched an attack. Almost immediately my view was obscured, the only thing visible a wall of blue sparks as the two fields met and opposed.

"The cage rattled, threatening to lift from the floor, and I felt like a laboratory rat caught in an experiment from which there would be no escape. The nuns pressed the attack harder, as if thrown into frenzy by my defiance of them. The sparks flew in an ever-increasing blaze of blue, so bright I had to press my eyelids tightly shut.

"To my dismay the temperature started to rise. At first it was almost imperceptible, but after a few more seconds of attack it became too obvious to ignore. The interior of the cage was heating up, fast.

"I leaned forward and threw the voltage up to its maximum. The sparks suddenly stopped and I opened my eyes to see the three figures recede away from the cage to the edges of the cellar where they drifted, as if unsure as to their next move. My defences had held… for now.

"The electrical hum from the cage thrummed all through my body and I felt slightly queasy. My head throbbed, a heavy pounding behind my left eye, but I knew my only chance of safety was to stay in the cage for as long as possible.

"But merely saving myself was not going to be enough. It seems my spirited defence had proved enough to dissuade the nuns from a further attack – but all I had achieved was diverting their attention for a time. As one they once again started to drift upwards towards the ceiling.

"I modulated the voltage, swinging it back and forth, but to no avail. They were now ignoring me completely. The white faces were already turned up to the ceiling, towards their goal – the old sleeping men in the dormitory.

"That I could not allow.

"I threw open the door to the cage and began to chant the first passage from the *Saaamaaa Ritual* where it refers to the expulsion of *Certayne Spyryts*."

Carnacki stopped unexpectedly. It was unusual for him to break a story in such a manner, and I was curious in the extreme to find the cause.

"I have stopped here because, in this adventure, I have come as close to my own death as at any other time," he said. "What I am about to relate happened, of that I am sure, but parts of it seem to me now almost dream-like, as if I was in some manner participating in a mere recording of events that had already transpired. If some of the following seems to go against all laws of sense and science, I apologize, but I can only tell you it as it happened and I have not yet got it straight in my own mind."

"Maybe this telling will prove the means for my own understanding."

"The nuns stopped their drift upwards and turned their attention back to me," he began again. "I had not stepped out of the cage, but the door was ajar, leaving me open to attack. Only the words of the ritual kept me from my doom. The incantation rang and echoed in the cellar. It had no discernible effect on the apparitions, but, at the least, I had halted their move towards the dormitory.

"We were now at an impasse, and one I had no idea of how to break.

"My choice was made for me as soon as I finished the chant. The nuns turned to face me, and once again pressed their attack. I only had enough time to throw myself back into the cage and pull the door closed before I was once more surrounded by a frenzy of blue sparks.

"I turned the voltage to full, but the attack faltered only slightly. There was a fury on these apparitions such that I had never seen. They threw themselves against the barrier of the cage, over and over, the cage creaking and rocking with each blow. Once again heat started to permeate inside, and soon I struggled to catch my breath, my very lungs feeling as if I was on fire.

"I believe I may have passed out, for the next thing I can remember with any clarity is drifting in blackness along a dark tunnel, the only light a red glow in the far distance towards which I was being inexorably drawn. I was aware of still being inside my cage, but somehow I was also here, in this tunnel, as if my being was split in two distinct parts.

"The red glow grew closer, and as it did so, the tunnel grew increasingly warm until the skin on my face tightened and once more I felt my eyebrows singe and I smelled burning hair.

"I found myself looking down on a conflagration in which three tall stakes stood inside a ring of flame. Pale faces looked on outside the fire as the nuns, tied as they were to the stakes, raised their faces and screamed to the skies. Flame reached for me, like long arms eager to draw me into a warm embrace. The burns on my throat flared anew, like a noose, ever-tightening.

"Only dimly aware of doing so, I kicked at the cage walls, even as I was drawn closer to the raging inferno. Heat seared my throat until I had no breath left and the red glow began to spread and cover everything inside me.

"I was about to give in to its enticing warmth when a cool breeze blew up, as if from nowhere, and a high singing called to me. I did not recognize the words, but I knew that I must obey. The fire receded into the dark even quicker than it had come as I sped back along the dark tunnel at a vertiginous speed. I came to a slamming stop back inside the cage – at the same instant as a donkey-kick from my right leg finally sprang open the door. I rolled out onto the welcoming cold of the cellar flagstones, gasping for air.

"It took me long seconds to realize I was alone in the rapidly cooling room.

"The singing voice that had dragged me from the flame still rang in my head and as I came to my senses I realized it came from the chapel above me, a high, almost operatic tune. As I lay there I recognized it, although I have never before heard it sung. It was the same invocation that I myself had tried to use earlier -- the first passage from the *Saaamaaa Ritual*. Up in the chapel, someone else was attempting a banishing."

"I leapt up the steps of the narrow staircase three at a time and arrived in a chapel that glowed in blue luminescence, as if seen through thick stained glass. The three white-faced nuns were once more attacking a psychic defence, but not one of my making.

"Someone had laid out a pentacle and protective circles in chalk on the chapel floor – a squat figure in a flowing blue robe with a cowl hanging over the face standing in the centre. It was from this figure that the song emanated – her voice echoing and soaring in every timber, ever nook and cranny of the high vaulted room.

"The nuns pressed an attack against the pentacle from three points. Sparks flew -- sending shadow and light dancing through the chapel like rapid lightning flashes. Throughout everything the singer kept up the incantation. As she approached the end of the first passage the nuns leapt into a prolonged attack. The robed singer involuntarily took a step backward and, even from this distance I saw where her foot crossed the line of the inner circle. The nun nearest her surged forward and the defender's voice faltered.

"If I did nothing, she would be dead in seconds and all hope of stopping the *entities* would be lost.

"I ran forward, shouting as I moved, taking up the chant from where she had dropped it. I leapt past the nun nearest to me, feeling a burst of searing heat at my calf before I tumbled into the pentacle.

"I had given the defender just enough time to step back into the relative safety of the defence's centre.

"Soon we had two voices raised in the chant, my thicker, courser tones in counter point to her high perfect pitch. As the incantation continued, so too did the nun's attacks, but I suddenly felt in total control, never in any danger of faltering. Although I have never tried to memorize it, I sang the incantation the whole way through to the end, and I did not miss a word or a beat.

"As we neared the finish a part of me wondered how this might end, for the nuns showed no sign of lessening their attack, and we had but eight bars of the song left in us.

"I need not have worried, for my partner was more prepared than even I could have imagined. When my own voice faltered and stopped at the end of the ritual, she kept right on going. I heard a thing that I have only ever heard on one other occasion.

The Unknown Last Line of the Saaamaaa Ritual was sung quite audibly in the room.

The chapel fell silent and the blue luminescence flared, just once. The figures of the nuns seemed to stretch and grow. Then it was as if a breeze blew through the chapel. The nuns fell apart into motes of swirling dust that was quickly dissipated leaving us alone in the quiet dark.

"The defender threw back her cowl and the *Matron* smiled

at me.

"'I don't stand for any nonsense in *my* hospital.'

"She was tight-lipped about things thereafter. I helped her clean the pentacle from the floor, for it would not do for any signs of our night's work to be found there in the chapel. She would not say how she knew of the *Sisters of Mercy* or where she received the training necessary for the banishment, but at the last I believe she let slip a clue.

"She had a twinkle in her eye as we parted.

"'Have you been at the hospital long?' I asked, probing for information.

"'My family has a long history of servitude hereabouts,' she replied.

"'I do not believe I ever caught your name,' I said.

"'Abigail Smith. That's Smith, with an 'i'.'

She smiled, and shooed me out of the door.

"Out you go," Carnacki said to us just five minutes later as he did some shooing of his own.

Jessop and I walked together along the north embankment. A fog was rolling in and when we found ourselves walking alongside the wall adjoining the Royal Infirmary Carnacki's story seemed all too real.

We hurried our pace somewhat.

A high singing voice carried across the hospital grounds, but we did not stop to listen, and we did not feel quite safe until the chapel, and the singer inside, was long behind us.

Further Reading

These were the first three stories I wrote back in 2009, and originally appeared in the now rare chapbook box set CARNACKI: GHOSTFINDER. They are reprinted here as an introduction to my take on William Hope Hodgson's character.

If you enjoyed these, you might enjoy my Carnacki collections, HEAVEN AND HELL, THE WATCHER AT THE GATE and THE EDINBURGH TOWNHOUSE.

I am a Scottish writer, now living in Canada, with over thirty novels published in the genre press and over 300 short story credits in thirteen countries.

I have books available from a variety of publishers including Dark Regions Press and Severed Press, and my work has appeared in a number of professional anthologies and magazines with recent sales to NATURE Futures, Penumbra and Buzzy Mag among others. I live in Newfoundland with whales, bald eagles and icebergs for company and when I'm not writing I drink beer, play guitar and dream of fortune and glory.

Willie
williammeikle.com

OTHER BOOKS BY WILLIAM MEIKLE

NOVELS

The S-Squad Series
Berserker
Crustaceans
Eldren: The Book of the Dark
Fungoid
Generations
Island Life
Night of the Wendigo
Ramskull
Sherlock Holmes: The Dreaming Man
Songs of Dreaming Gods
The Boathouse
The Creeping Kelp
The Dunfield Terror
The Exiled
The Green and the Black
The Hole
The Invasion
The Midnight Eye Files: The Amulet
The Midnight Eye Files: The Sirens
The Midnight Eye Files: The Skin Game
The Ravine
The Valley
The Concordances of the Red Serpent
Watchers: The Battle for the Throne
Watchers: The Coming of the King
Watchers: Culloden
The Road Hole Bunker Mystery
Dagger of the Martyrs (With Steven Savile)
Hound of Night / Veil Knights #2 (as Rowan Casey)

NOVELLAS

Broken Sigil
Clockwork Dolls
Pentacle
Professor Challenger: The Island of Terror
Sherlock Holmes: Revenant
Sherlock Holmes: The London Terrors (3 novella omnibus)
The House on the Moor
The Job
The Midnight Eye Files: Deal or No Deal
The Plasm
The CopyCat Murders
Tormentor

SHORT STORY COLLECTIONS

Carnacki: Heaven and Hell
Carnacki: The Edinburgh Townhouse
Carnacki: The Watcher at the Gate
Dark Melodies
Myth and Monsters
Professor Challenger: The Kew Growths
Samurai and Other Stories
Sherlock Holmes: The Quality of Mercy
The Ghost Club
Home From the Sea
Into The Black
Flower of Scotland
Augustus Seton: Collected Chronicles
Bug Eyed Monsters

Details of all of these works and more can be found at his website at
williammeikle.com

Printed in Great Britain
by Amazon